ARNO AND HIS HORSE

Jane Godwin & Felicita Sala

SCRIBBLE

For Mitch,
who brings love, friendship, family.
JG

For Emma and Junie, with love.
FS

The illustrations in this book are made with watercolour, gouache and coloured pencils.
Typeset in Adobe Caslon

Scribble, an imprint of Scribe Publications
18–20 Edward Street, Brunswick, Victoria 3056, Australia
2 John Street, Clerkenwell, London, WC1N 2ES, United Kingdom
3754 Pleasant Ave, Suite 100, Minneapolis, Minnesota 55409 USA

Text © Jane Godwin 2020
Illustrations © Felicita Sala 2020

First published by Scribble 2020

This book is printed on FSC certified paper from responsibly managed forests, ensuring that
the supply chain from forest to end-user is chain of custody certified. Printed and bound in
China by 1010.

9781925849486 (ANZ hardback)
9781912854899 (UK hardback)
9781950354467 (North American hardback)

Catalogue records for this title are available from the National Library of Australia and the
British Library.

scribblekidsbooks.com
@scribblekidsbooks

Arno had a horse,
it was brown and it was black.

He took it with him everywhere,
but did he bring it back?

Back along the riverbed
we sifted through the sand,
then we searched for Arno's little horse
all across the land.

'Are you sure you left it here?'
asked Mercy with a frown.
'I can't remember,' Arno whispered,
'where I put it down…'

We looked in our house,
with the fort and the swings.
We didn't find the horse,
but we found some other things.

Back to the playground,
we climbed up the tree.
We looked over the country
as far as we could see.

Back to the bush,
we ran from here to there.

Mercy said, "Your little horse,
it could be *anywhere*!"

Back to the store
with the apples and the corn,
we found a lot of stuff to buy.
The horse? It was still gone.

Back to the field
where we'd played with some boys,
we looked in the shed
and we tipped out all the toys.

The last thing we found
was a ball that was flat.
"Okay," said Dad,
"we're done,
that's that."

"Can't you play with something else?
The frisbee? Your toy train?"

But this was Arno's favorite thing.
He couldn't quite explain
the feel of it upon his hand,
and all the different ways
the little horse reminded him
of other, far-off days.

And of things his grandpa told him
'bout the old times long ago,
rode his horse across the river
when the river was in flow.

Grandpa made the toy for him,
he'd carved it out of wood.
"We need to find it," Arno said,
"I really think we should."

It had big eyes, a peaceful face,
made Arno's mind feel light.
He thought of his horse every day,
he dreamt of it at night.

Arno asked his grandpa,
he asked him in his dreams.
"Can you see it, Grandpa?
Can you bring it back to me?"

And do you know, that little horse
was deep, deep down below,
and in the night, it started up
with quite a way to go.

Down along the river now,
past tall trees, under stars,
the little horse, it journeyed on
around the sleeping cars.

In bed, Arno was dreaming
of holding Grandpa's hand,
walking down the riverbed,
drawing in the sand.

And in the dream he somehow saw
the horse from long ago,
his grandpa riding bareback
when the river was in flow.

His grandpa rode from bank to bank,
brave and strong and free.
He wasn't frail, or sick, or sad,
but how he used to be.

Arno raced out in the night,
the stars gone from the river.
But in their place, the night shone bright
and he could see for ever.

He knew now where his horse would be,
just near the longest bridge.
He ran along the gravel road
until he reached the ridge.

And there it was! His special horse!
It was a little battered.
But as he'd hoped, the horse came back—

and that was all that mattered.